Winnie
AND Wilbur

Mrs Parmar

The Little Ordinaries

WINN
Goes for
Gold

The Head Teacher

Jerry the Giant

The Baby

Στο Cαφενείο Μηνάς – Κ.Π.
(To Cafeneo Menas)
For all those who, like me, are never going to win a gold
medal, but still enjoy having a go at things – xx

## OXFORD
UNIVERSITY PRESS

Great Clarendon Street, Oxford OX2 6DP

Oxford University Press is a department of the University of Oxford.
It furthers the University's objective of excellence in research, scholarship,
and education by publishing worldwide. Oxford is a registered trade mark of
Oxford University Press in the UK and in certain other countries

Database right Oxford University Press (maker)

First published in 2012
First published in this edition 2019

British Library Cataloguing in Publication Data
Data available

ISBN: 978-0-19-277495-8

2 4 6 8 10 9 7 5 3 1

Printed in India by Manipal Technologies Limited

Paper used in the production of this book is a natural,
recyclable product made from wood grown in sustainable forests.
The manufacturing process conforms to the environmental
regulations of the country of origin.

LAURA OWEN & KORKY PAUL

# Winnie AND Wilbur

# WINNIE
Goes for
Gold

OXFORD
UNIVERSITY PRESS

# CONTENTS

# WINNIE
## Minds the Baby

# WINNIE
## Goes for Gold

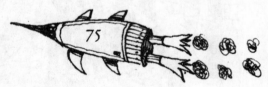

# WINNIE'S
## House Party

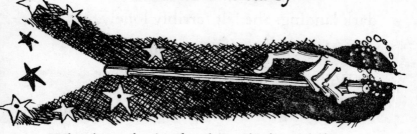

Winnie woke in the deep dark middle
of the night, clutching her tatty batty
blankets and listening to the darkness,
and wondered what had woken her.

Silence.

There should have been a sound of
Wilbur snuffling and grunting.

'Wilbur?' Winnie picked up her wand.
**swish!** *'Abracadabra!'* The end of the
wand glowed like a torch, which scribbled

light around the room. Winnie shuffled
into her slip-sloppers, pulled on her
messing gown, and set off along the long
dark landing. She felt terribly lonely,
all on her only in that big house.

'Wilbur?'

Winnie opened door after door, but the
only answer she got back from the empty
rooms was her own echo.

'Where are you?' said Winnie.

'Where are you?' said the echo.

'I'm here, you fool!' said Winnie.

'I'm here, you fool!' said the echo.

**Crash!**

'What was that?'

Winnie hurried downstairs to the

kitchen and shone her wand-torch . . .

'Wilbur, there you are!'

'Mnmnmeeow,' said Wilbur, licking his lips.

'Heck, Wilbur! You've cooked more than we could eat in a week!' said Winnie.'Right, that's it!'

'Meeow?'

'We're going to have a house party!'

'Me-he-he!' laughed Wilbur.

'Not a party for houses! That would be as silly as a snail taking up clog dancing. A party for people in our house. We've got empty rooms and too much food. And I'd like people to talk to instead of just cats and echoes.'

'Mrrow!' scowled Wilbur.

10

So Winnie raced around her house,
magicking rooms ready for guests.

'*Abracadabra!*'

Cobweb curtains appeared.

'*Abracadabra!*'

There were suddenly toad-plump
cushions, vases of thistles, slug-slime soaps
in plastic packets, and more.

'Our guests will be as snug as a whole
termite hill of bugs!' said Winnie.

'*Abracadabra!*' Winnie magicked herself a magnificent party dress. 'Now we just need to plan an itinerararerary.

'Meeow?'

'It's a list of what we'll do and when we'll do it,' said Winnie. 'You'll have to write it down, Wilbur.'

# ·ITINERARARERARY·

8.00am Guests arrive. Show
them to their rooms.

9.00am Breakfast.

10.00am Play hide and seek
in the garden.

1.00pm Picnic lunch

2.00pm Games with bats
(from the battery)
and balls.

6.00pm Supper

7.00pm Watch dVd
'Witch Upon a Star'

8.00pm Bedtime

14

'There!' said Winnie, pinning the
itinerararerary to the fridge. Her
witch-watch said it was eight o'clock
already. 'Where is everyone?' said
Winnie. 'Oh, whoops! I've not invited
them yet!'

Winnie tapped buttons on her telling moan to call her sisters Wilma and Wanda and Wendy, and her Uncle Owen, her Auntie Alice, and her Cousin Cuthbert. She invited them all to her party, and they all texted back 'yes'. They forgot to add 'please', which Winnie thought was rather rude. And they all asked if they could bring friends along with them, which Winnie thought was even ruder. But she said, 'Oh, all right then.'

**Bing-bong!** They all arrived.

'Meet Carol,' said Uncle Owen.

'Allow me to introduce Zane, Stig, and Fang,' said Cousin Cuthbert.

'This is Clemency,' said Auntie Alice. 'I'm not sharing a room with her, mind.'

Luckily Winnie's house was big enough to have rooms for everyone, not that any

of them were happy with what they got.

'I wanted a sea view,' said Wilma.

'But we aren't anywhere near the sea!' said Winnie.

'Humph,' went Wilma.

'Can't we have bunk beds?' said Cuthbert.

'This pillow is lumpy!' said Carol.

'Oh, for goosy-gander's big fat panda's sake, let's have breakfast,' said Winnie.

It got worse at breakfast. Cuthbert said,
'You know why they call it breakfast?'

'Why?'

'Because it's when you break things,
fast!' he said. And he picked up his snereal
bowl and threw it onto the floor—**smash!**

And soon—**rip! crash! splinter!**—
Winnie's guests were having a smashing
time, breaking her things. They were
behaving very badly.

'Come into the garden!' said Winnie. But they went on behaving badly in magical ways. **Pow! Zip! Zap! Zlop! Zing! Croak!** Magic was flying off wands all over the place. Winnie ducked. 'Er . . .' she said, 'we must play hide and seek now. It's on the itinerararerary!'

'Bagsy I'm "it",' said Wendy. 'Everybody hide while I count to a hundred. One—tickle flea, two—tickle flea, three . . .'

Winnie's guests hid here, there and everywhere.

Winnie dug her way into the smelly compost pile of old leaves and peelings and rottings. It was soft and warm and buzzing with flies.

'This is nice!' said Winnie, settling into
the quiet smelly warmth.

But, as her witch-watch ticked on,
Winnie could hear chatting and laughing.
'They've found everyone except me. Clever
me!' she said. Then it went quiet. 'Hey!'
called Winnie. She climbed out of the
compost and stomped inside . . . where her
guests were causing havoc!

Winnie was dripping with muck. Her
guests looked at her and were about to laugh
when Winnie put her hands on her hips.

'You are all so RUDE!' she shouted.

And everyone froze.

'I don't want you at my party any longer,' said Winnie. 'Go home. NOW!'

'But the itinerararerary says food and films and . . .' began Aunt Alice.

Winnie was wondering if they would all refuse to go, when . . .

# Thump, thump, thump!

Winnie looked over her shoulder, and saw Jerry coming through the garden. She turned back to her guests.

'If you don't all go home now, I'll get my big brother onto you!'

'What big brother?' asked her guests (especially her sisters).

'My big brother, Jerry. Look!' Winnie pointed. 'There he is!'

24

Thump, thump!

'Can I borrow a cup of sugar, please, Missus?' said Jerry.

'He's big, isn't he?' said Winnie.

Winnie's guests gasped. They grabbed their bags and they tumbled out of the house and away.

25

'Thanks, Jerry!' said Winnie. 'Will you stay for tea?'

It was nice sitting and chatting and scrunching and slurping and burping with just Jerry and Scruff and Wilbur, with no itinerararerary and no magic.

When Jerry and Scruff went home,
Winnie soaked the compost off in a nice
bath of fresh frogspawn bubbles. Then she
and Wilbur settled back in their own old
bed as the empty house settled to silence
around them.

'Goodnight, my lovely,' said Winnie.

'Goodnight, my lovely,' said her echo.

'Purrrrrr!' said Wilbur.

And that was just enough company.

# WINNIE'S
## Pedal Power

**Creep-creep-creep.** A bush with leaves and black hair and a long nose and a strange stripy double trunk was scuttling across Winnie's garden. **Rustle-creep!**

'Tweet?' went a pretty little bird. Then, 'Meeow!' **Pounce!**

'Tweet-tweetety-TWEET!' Flip-flap-flutter!

'Wilbur, you BAD cat!' The bush wagged a twig at Wilbur. 'Were you going

to eat that pretty fountain-tailed spotted
nit-catcher?'

'Mrrow.' Wilbur looked at his claws.

'Huh!' puffed the bush. 'Well, I'm
going to make a bird table that is too high
for you to reach, and then the birdies will
be safe!' The bush waved a wand twig.
'Abracadabra!'

And instantly there appeared a very big
bird table mounted high on a greasy pole.

'Try climbing that!' said Winnie-
the-bush.

**Scrabble-scrabble** went Wilbur.
**Slip-slide. Splat-cat!**

'Hee-hee!' laughed Winnie. 'Now all
the birdies in the world can come and visit
me and not get pounced on.'

Back in her house, Winnie took a dusty
musty fusty old book off a shelf. It was
Great-Grandma Wilhelmina's Big Book
of Birdies. She put a tick beside the
fountain-tailed spotted nit-catcher.

'Now I want to see all those other
birdies. We need food for that birdie table.'

Winnie and Wilbur put small seeds and
ants' ankles and wasps' warts onto the bird
table, then they hid. Soon—**flippety-
flap**—down came wrens and hoppit-
poppets and finches and plumed plumps.
Winnie put more ticks in her Big Book
of Birdies. **Tick, tick, tick!**

'We need different food to attract
different birdies,' said Winnie. So she and
Wilbur got out spades and dug nice fresh
wiggling worms and slithering snails and
bumbling beetles.

'Num-yum!' said Winnie, trying some.
'Lucky birds!' And—**flap-flap-
flump**—down came pigeons and frumples
and blackbirds and screech-wimpers.
Winnie put more ticks in her book.

Next they put dead critters and
snake-cake and chilli biscuits onto the bird
table. *Neeeow-flop!* Down thudded
eagles and hoot-ninnies and condors and
wobble-wings.

'Look out!' said Winnie as a great galumphing ostrich came crashing along to gobble food off the ground under the bird table. **Tick, tick,** went Winnie. 'That's all of them spotted . . . oh! Except for a dodo. Why haven't we seen a dodo?'

Winnie waited with her big pencil all ready to tick . . . but time went on . . . and on . . . and on . . . and no dodo came.

'Perhaps dodos are particular about how they eat,' said Winnie. So they hang-dangled some of these. Sprinkled some of those. They even set a table with a knife and fork. Flocks of other birds came— **squawk-peep-chirrup-kraaak-chirp-cuckoo-quack!**—but still no dodo.

It was getting cold and dark.

'Botherarmarations!' said Winnie. 'We'd better go inside and I'll cook us some spossages.'

Winnie turned on the lights and heaters and the oven and the television. And there was a woman who was just saying, 'Of course, dodos are extinct . . .'

'Dodo's stink?' said Winnie, getting excited. 'Oo, I like a good stink!'

38

But the telly woman went on, 'The last dodos were hunted and eaten over three hundred years ago. Now they are gone for ever.'

'Oh, no!' said Winnie. 'Poor dodos! Naughty blooming cats eating them all!'

'It was people who killed the dodos,' said the telly woman.

'People!' said Winnie.

But the telly woman was still talking. 'And people will make other birds and animals extinct unless we stop cutting down forests for fuel. We must use less fuel to save our lovely . . .'

Winnie jumped up. 'Turn everything off that uses power, Wilbur!'

**Bop!** Off went the telly. **Click!** Off went the fire. **Snap!** Off went the lights.

'Mrrrow!' went Wilbur as Winnie stood on his tail.

'We must save the world for the lovely birdies and animals!' said Winnie.

**Brrr!** It was early for bed, but it was cold and dark, and they couldn't cook splossages without the oven on.

**Bump! Crash!** They went upstairs and jumped into bed. But Winnie stayed wide awake, thinking, and feeling hungry. Suddenly she sat up. 'I've got a blooming brilliant idea to save the birdies! Come on, Wilbur!'

Winnie and Wilbur fumbled their way out into the silvery moonlit garden.

'We need invention sorts of things,' said Winnie. They collected old wheels and chairs and cogs and chains and wires and tubes and pedals and planks and clocks.

'Stand back!' Winnie waved her wand. *Abracadabra!*

**Clatter-CRASH!** In a puff of magic, the bits all came together.

'Meeow?' asked Wilbur.

'It'll make electricity without polluting!' said Winnie. 'Hop on, let's get pedalling!'

**Clank!** The machine began to churn.

**Zap!** Lights flickered on inside the house.

'This is brilliant!' said Winnie. **Puff! Pant!** But, 'Heck in a handbag, however will I cook those splossages in the kitchen at the same time as being out here and pedalling the power to make the oven hot? Ooo, my poor old legs are turning to soggy spaghetti. I can't keep . . . Oh!'

45

Suddenly, strangely, stupendously the garden was lit up with a flickering glowing light. 'Cooer!' Winnie looked around in wonder.

'Mrrow!' Wilbur pointed. A most beautiful orange traily-feathery bird was flying down through the sky.

'It's a blooming phoenix!' said Winnie. 'And it's come for the chilli biscuits I put on the bird table!'

Winnie and Wilbur got down off their contraption. They stood and watched in wonder as the huge orange-red-gold bird settled to feed on their bird table, setting the table alight so that it lit the garden like a great torch.

'Nice and warming!' said Winnie.

People in the village saw the fire.

'It's a bonfire party!'

Children got out of bed. The grown-ups switched off their lights and their televisions and their radios and took their children over to Winnie's house.

'Wow!' they said when they saw the
phoenix. Then the phoenix began to sing
a strange, wild, haunting song. Winnie
drummed a beat with her wand and
everyone started dancing by the light of
the flames until their legs ached.

So Winnie waved her wand again.
'Abracadabra!' to turn her generator into
a massage chair for all those tired legs.

'Mine are still tired from pedalling!' said
Winnie. And she was first to try the
massage chair with Wilbur.

So because everyone in the village had come to Winnie's phoenix party, instead of sitting at home with their lights and televisions and radios on, Winnie had (sort of) saved the world.

'I'm glad we did our bit to help the animals and birdies,' said Winnie, 'even though I never did get to see a dodo.'

# WINNIE
## Minds the Baby

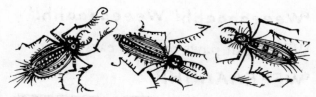

'What shall we do with this nice sunny day, eh, Wilbur?'

Winnie was leaning on her garden gate, scuffing her shoes in the dust and poking woodlice with her wand. 'How about a picnic? We could dangle our feet in the stinky swamp and nibble beetle bites and drink frothy pink burp-slurp pop. We could even . . .'

**'Weeeaaaahh!'** came a noise from

down the road.

'That sounds like you did yesterday, Wilbur, when I stamped on your tail because I thought it was a hairy snake.'

**'Weeeaaaahh! Weeeaaaahh!'**

Wilbur put paws over his ears.

**'WEEEAAAHH!'**

'Pickled parsnips, it's getting louder!' said Winnie. And just then, round the corner, came a lady pushing a pram.

'You want to get those wheels oiled,' said Winnie.

'Oh, it's not the wheels. It's my baby,' said the lady. 'He won't stop crying!'

'Really?' said Winnie, and she peered
down at the very cross baby.

'Coochie-coo!' said Winnie.

The baby stopped mid-wail, and gawped
at Winnie's witchy face, smiling at him.

'Biggle-boggle!' said Winnie, and she
blew a raspberry.

Chuckle, went the baby.

'Goodness!' said the lady. 'You made him laugh! Oh, Winnie, you're a wonder with babies!'

'**Goo-goo,**' said the baby.

'That's all he can say at the moment,' said the lady. 'Just "**goo-goo**" and "**weeeaaaah**". Oh, I'm so tired!'

'Why don't you go and have a snozzle-snooze in my hammock?' said Winnie. 'Wilbur and I can babysit.'

'That's very kind of you,' said the lady. 'But do you know how to look after babies? They need feeding. And their nappies need changing.'

'Easy-peazy, squashed-worm squeezy,' said Winnie. 'You don't need to worry about a thing.'

58

So the baby's mummy climbed into the
hammock and was soon snoring happily.

'What shall we do with you?' Winnie
asked the baby. 'Shall we go for a picnic?'

**'Goo!'** said the baby.

Winnie hurled pickled pepper and
sprout sandwiches into a basket. She added
a bottle of pink burp-slurp pop and a
packet of cabbage and caterpillar crisps.
'That's for you and me, Wilbur. Now,
what would the baby like? Worms?'
Winnie added a jar of baby pink worms.
Then they set off to the park.

In the park, Winnie lifted the baby from
his pram and sat him on a rug, and they
ate lunch. The baby loved the juicy little
worms.

'Goo-goo!'
He loved being swung by Wilbur.
'Goo-goo!'
Winnie loved swinging too. Swing-
swong, swing-swong!

'**Wheee!**' went Winnie, tipping back
to make the swing go higher. Her hat fell
off. '**Wheee!**' went Winnie again. 'I'm
going to kick the clouds and see if they
bounce!' What she did kick was her shoe
up into the air so that it crashed down—
**splat!**—onto someone else's picnic.

'**Goo-goo!**' laughed the baby.

'Let's try the see-saw!' said Winnie. She sat down hard on one end and catapulted Wilbur into the air.

'**Goo-goo,**' laughed the baby. Then suddenly, '**Weeeaaaahh!**' cried the baby.

'Ooer,' said Winnie. She patted the baby on the head. 'What's the matter diddums?'

'**Weeeaaaahh!**' went the baby.

63

'Are you hungry? Have another worm,' said Winnie. 'Thirsty? Have some burp-slurp to drink.'

**Hiccup! Burp! 'Weeeaaaahh!'** went the baby.

Wilbur pointed at the baby's bottom and held his nose.

'He needs a new nappy, does he?' said Winnie, making a face. 'I haven't got any. Do you think leaves and moss would do?'

It was a smelly job, but they did it.

**'Weeeaaaahh!'** went the baby, on and on.

'Whatever else can the matter be?' said Winnie. 'Does he need a sleep?' Winnie picked up the baby. 'I'll sing the song Great-Auntie Winifred used to sing to me when I was 'iccle:

Close your eyes, 'iccle baby,

close your eyes, 'iccle boy.

Don't be weepy, just be sleepy,

Close your eyes now, 'iccle boy.'

**'Weeeaaaahh!'** went the baby.

'Well, that didn't work, did it?' said

Winnie.

Wilbur held his tail over his ears.

'Perhaps he's bored,' said Winnie.

Winnie waved her wand. 'Abracadabra!'

And instantly the ducks from the pond
and the squirrels from the trees came and
danced for the baby.

'**Weeeaaaahh!**' went the baby.

'Oh, for grated gherkins' sake!' said
Winnie. 'I wish you could talk, little baby,
and TELL us what it is you DO want
instead of just going "**weeeaaaahh**" to
everything!'

That gave Winnie an idea. 'Abracadabra!'
The baby paused for a moment. 'Er . . .
good afternoon!' he said. He looked just as
surprised as Winnie and Wilbur were to hear
real words coming out of his mouth.

'There!' said Winnie. 'No more crying, eh?
Just tell us what you need to keep you happy!'

'Well, where shall I begin?' said the baby.
He waved an arm in an expressive way, which
made him tumble over, and he couldn't get
up again. 'Dear, oh dear,' he said. 'I . . . er . . .
**weeeaaaahh** . . . I mean, I wish that
I could sit up properly, and walk about like
you do.'

'No problem-o,' said Winnie.
'Abracadabra!'

And instantly the baby was up and
running, chasing ducks and squirrels,
snatching at feathers and tails, and trying
to eat them.

'Catch the baby!' said Winnie. But the
baby was fast, even though his leaf and
moss nappy was sagging around his knees.

'Good afternoon!' he called to surprised
passers-by as he ran. Winnie and Wilbur
and the pram ran after him.

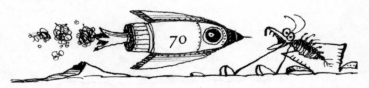

'We must give him back to his mummy,'
panted Winnie. 'Chase him over there!'

They caught the baby just as they got to
Winnie's garden gate.

'I don't want to be picked up!' said the
baby, struggling in Winnie's arms. 'Oh,
look, it's my mummy!'

Winnie could see the baby's mummy
waking up. 'Quick, *Abracadabra!*' she said.

Instantly the baby was back to normal,
but with a very surprised look on his face.

'Hello, darling!' said the lady. 'Thank you
so much, Winnie. Was he any trouble?'

'Er . . .' said Winnie.

'What have you been up to?' the lady
asked her baby.

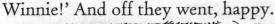

'**Gurgle-wurgle-boggle-boo!**'

'I do believe you've taught him to talk,
Winnie!' And off they went, happy.

'Wilbur,' said Winnie, 'when DO babies say their first words? Without magic.'

'Meeow,' shrugged Wilbur.

'Well, I hope this baby forgets all about today before he learns to talk and tell his mummy about it!' said Winnie.

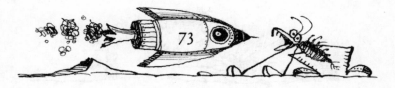

# WINNIE
## Goes for Gold

Winnie and Wilbur were wearing large
veiled hats and gloves and suits and boots.

**Buzzzzzz!** went the bees in a dark
cloud around Winnie. **Puff-puff!** went
Wilbur's smoke machine to make the bees
sleepy. **Cough-cough, buzz-buzz,**
went Winnie, Wilbur, and the bees.

'This is the best honey in the world!'
said Winnie. 'Collected from our own
pongwort trumpet flowers and tasting like

nothing you've ever had from a honey jar before!'

The frames of honeycomb that Winnie lifted dripping and dribbling from the hive didn't look like any honey you've ever had from a jar, either. This honey was purple, and it fizzed.

'Oo, Wilbur, we can have honeyed cockroach crunch biscuits, and honey spread on nuffins, and . . . oh, I've gone and forgotten the jars, and now I've got honey dripping into my boots.'

**Buzzzzzz! Bing bing!**

'Eh?' said Winnie. 'Whoever heard of bees saying "bing"?'

'Meeow!' Wilbur pointed.

'Oh, it's my blooming mobile moan!'
said Winnie. 'How am I meant to answer it
when my hands are all sticky?'

**BUZZZZZZ! BING!**

'Wait a minute!' said Winnie, trying
to dig out her phone at the same time as
holding a frame full of sticky goo with
bees buzzing all around it. She lifted the
phone to her ear. 'Who is it?' she said. 'I'm
buzzy. I mean busy.' There was a pause.

'Oh, it's you, Mrs P. You sound a bit
flustered.' Pause. 'Oh, I see. Mmm. Yes.'
Pause. 'I've got just what you need! Fresh
as anything! I'll just put it into something
other than my boots, and I'll be there.
Don't you worry, Mrs P. The little
ordinaries will have their honey tea!'

'Meeow?' asked Wilbur as Winnie tried and tried to put down the phone that was honey-stuck to her hand.

'It's school Sports Day,' said Winnie. 'They've got scones for the tea but no honey to put on them. Right, I need a good big jar. Where's my wand?' Winnie waved her wand. *Abracadabra!'*

And instantly there appeared a big
Greek jar decorated with people running
and jumping and fighting and throwing
javelins and discuses and wrestling.

'Oo, just right for Sports Day!' said
Winnie. 'Look, Wilbur! It's the Olympic
Games. That's an extra special sort of
Sports Day from the olden days.'

### Pour, lick, slurp! Buzzzzzz!

Winnie and Wilbur got the honey into the jar ... and all over their gloves and suits ... as the bees told them what they thought of honey thieves. **Buzzzzzz!**

'Come on!' said Winnie, trying to peel off her gloves and hat and suit at the same time as carrying the jar to the school.

Winnie and Wilbur jogged with the jar
to the school field where loudspeakers
were announcing:

'Year Three egg-and-spoon race to the
starting line, please!'

'Egg-and-spoon race!' said Winnie,
stopping still in the middle of the field.

'Ah, there you are!' said Mrs Parmar, hurrying over. 'Bring the honey to the tea tent, please.'

'But that's not right,' said Winnie. 'They didn't do egg-and-spoon races at the Olympic Games.'

'This isn't the Olympics!' said Mrs Parmar. 'Oh, good gracious, whatever . . .'

**BUZZZZZZ!**

The bees had caught up with Winnie and their stolen honey.

**Buzzzzzz!**

'Run!' said Mrs Parmar.

Winnie ran.

She ran fast around the race track.

'Yay! Well done, Winnie!' shouted the children.

'Drop the honey jar!' shouted the parents, which was a good idea, but Winnie wasn't listening.

**Buzzzzzz!**

Winnie jumped over the tug-of-war rope.

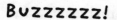

**Buzzzzzz!**

'DROP THE HONEY JAR!'

Winnie wasn't listening. She hurdled over pushchairs.

**Buzzzzzz!**

'DROP THE . . .' But it was no good.

There was the table full of prize cups, and the bees were getting closer every moment! Winnie waved her wand.

'Abracadabra!' And instantly her wand became very long and bendy, so that— **boing!**—Winnie pole-vaulted right over the prizes table and the headmaster.

'Hooray!' shouted the children.

**Buzzzzzz!**

'DROP THE JAR!' shouted the grown-ups. But—**splash!**—Winnie landed in the swimming pool. **Paddle, paddle, paddle!** went Winnie.

'Yippeeee!' shouted the children.

**Buzzzzzz!** went the bees very loudly in Winnie's ears as she staggered from the pool, too tired to run any more.

'DROP THE JAR!'

And this time Winnie heard.

With an almighty effort she hurled that
jar of honey just as far as she could
. . . which wasn't very far at all . . . and—
**smash!**—it became a pile of sticky
pottery pieces covered in bees.

'The honey is running away!' wailed
Winnie.

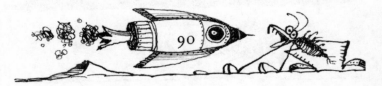

She waved her wand. *'Abracadabra!'*

And instantly bits of jar and dollops of honey spun into a blur, and then settled back together, looking like . . . this.

'Oh dear,' said Winnie.

'Put the jar on the table with the others,' said Mrs Parmar. 'It's time for the prizes, and then for tea.'

There were cups for this, and certificates for that. 'What about this one?' asked the headmaster, pointing at Winnie's jar.

'I believe it depicts the ancient Olympic Games,' said Mrs Parmar.

'Who has won it?' asked the headmaster.

'Winnie has,' said Mrs Parmar. 'She ran, jumped, hurdled, vaulted and swam faster and further than anybody else today.'

'HOORAY!' shouted the children.

'At the ancient Olympic Games,' explained the headmaster, 'they gave winners a crown of laurel leaves. Today they give gold medals.'

'That sounds nice!' said Winnie. So Wilbur wove her a pongwort trumpet-leaf crown. The only gold was the honey that Winnie licked from her sticky fingers.

At tea they talked about sports from the olden days.

'Throw your empty plates across the field,' said Winnie. 'See who can get them the furthest. That's what they're doing on my jar.'

Soon there were people running with cupcakes on their noses, hopping with their shopping, hurling handbags, and all sorts.

'You can see why the Olympics caught on, can't you!' said Winnie to Wilbur. She was too tired and too full of tea to do any more racing or hurling herself, but she was having fun.

That night, Winnie put her cracked and stuck-together jar by her bed. The athletes were still running round it. They made Winnie feel dizzy, then dozy, then snoozy. **Snore!**

She dreamed of driving a chariot pulled by a giant Wilbur and chased by bees.

Z Z Z Z Z₀₀₀

Enjoy more magic moments with
**Winnie** AND **Wilbur**